WOLF TALES

WOLF TALES

Native American Children's Stories

Edited and Adapted for Children
by
Mary Powell

Illustrated by
Deborah Reade

Ancient City Press
Santa Fe, New Mexico

Grateful acknowledgement is made to Mrs. Allan Macfarlan for permission to use "The Tired Wolf" and "Prince of the Wolves." Both tales were included in her late husband's book *Fireside Book of North American Indian Tales*.

International Standard Book Number: 0-941270-73-4
Library of Congress Catalog Number: 92-073573

Book design by Mary Powell

Cover illustration and design by Deborah Reade
Story illustrations by Deborah Reade

Library of Congress Cataloging-in-Publication Data

Wolf tales : Native American children's stories / compiled and edited
  by Mary Powell ; illustrations by Deborah Reade. — 1st ed.
        p.   cm.
    Summary: A collection of legends from the Cherokee, Dakota Sioux,
  and other Indian trides, centering around the spiritual power of the
  wolf and its interaction with man and other animals.
      ISBN 0-941270-73-4 : $8.95
      1. Indians of North America — Legends. 2. Wolves — Folklore-
  -Juvenile literature. [1. Indians of North America — Legends.
  2. Wolves — Folklore.] I. Powell, Mary, 1942-   . II. Reade,
  Deborah, ill.
  E98.F6W8 1992
  398.24'52974442 —   92-29690
                                                                  CIP
                                                                   AC

10 9 8 7 6 5 4

CONTENTS

A NOTE TO READERS

The tales in this book were collected in the field by anthropologists and have been retold as authentically as possible. Although they have been adapted for children, they retain some of the syntax and sound of the oral tradition from which they were taken. From them, the reader can learn the kind of narrative constructions that a Native American storyteller uses in crafting and weaving a tale. Children will then be able to experience language as performance as well as literature. Enjoy!

INTRODUCTION

For Native Americans the earth and everything on it is a huge living web. This web includes the relationships of people to each other and with animals. To Native Americans animals are not lesser beings. Instead they are relatives—brothers and sisters—of human beings. People and animals share many ways of being together. Animals live in tribes just as humans do. Some Native Americans call these tribes "The Four-Footed Tribes." As you will see in some of the tales in this book, the four-footed ones hold their own councils, have relatives among other animal tribes, and often provide special help to their human relatives.

Some members of the Four-Footed Tribes have been more important to Native Americans than others. One animal that has held a special place for almost every tribe is the wolf. We know an important relationship must have existed between early humans and wolves because of the domestic dogs we now have as pets. Fifteen thousand years ago, wolves probably lived very close to humans. They shared food with them and eventually came to live in their villages. These tame wolves became our sheep dogs, collies, and other dog breeds.

Indians have always been keen observers of nature. They saw that wolves were unusually intelligent animals. They admired them for their strength and speed and their great powers of endurance. Wolf families lived together like human families. Mothers and fathers, cubs, single aunts and uncles and sometimes even orphan cubs lived in large family groups and shared dens. Wolves knew how to do many things cooperatively. They hunted together and took turns taking care of the cubs. No wonder Native Americans admired these courageous animals and wanted to learn their skills.

Indians continue to have a close connection with wolves in the wild. All the stories in this book describe this special bond. The tales we have from Native Americans are stories that were told aloud, handed down from parents to children for hundreds of years. Some of these tales teach lessons, and some describe wolves' magical and healing powers. Many of these stories are still told today and, as you will see, wolves have much to teach us.

WOLF TALES

THE WOLF AND THE TURTLE

Cherokee

The god Kanati had wolves who hunted for him. Wolves were known to be good hunters and they never failed to find meat. Once he sent out two wolves at a time. One went to the east and never returned. The other went to the north. When he returned at night and did not find his fellow brother, he knew his brother must be in trouble. He went to look for him, and after traveling for some time he found his brother nearly dead beside a great green snake which had bitten him.

The snake itself was too badly wounded to crawl away. The angry wolf with his magic powers took out several hairs of his own whiskers and shot them into the body of the snake.

Then he hurried back to Kanati who sent his friend the turtle to find the great doctor—who lived in the west—to save the wounded wolf. The other wolf went back to help his brother and by his magic powers cured him long

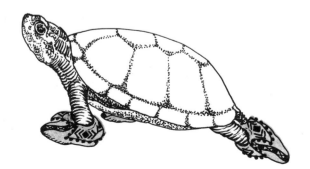

before the doctor came from the west. The turtle was such a slow traveler, and the doctor had taken too much time preparing the medicine. Now the injured wolf recovered thanks to his brother.

The Cherokee Indians originally lived in the mountainous areas of what is now Virginia, North Carolina, South Carolina, and in parts of Tennessee, Georgia, and Alabama. They now live in North Carolina and Oklahoma.

3

THE WOLF
AND THE
OMAHA WARRIOR
Omaha

Many years ago a large war party of Pawnee Indians raided the Cheyennes. The Cheyenne Indians were camped on one of the branches of the Arkansas River. After capturing the Cheyenne horses and fleeing, an old Omaha warrior who had joined the Pawnee became sick from an old leg wound. That night he stole away from his companions to take another route home.

One morning as the Omaha warrior was riding along at a slow pace he noticed a wolf trotting ahead of him. The wolf was looking back at him now and then to see

if the warrior was still moving. When the man hobbled his horse and camped, the wolf sat nearby watching every movement of the sick warrior.

In the morning when the warrior continued his travels, the wolf trotted ahead as before. Suddenly, in the afternoon, the wolf drew his tail between his legs and fled into a deep ravine. The man hurriedly looked around but saw nothing. The Omaha

warrior went into
the ravine to hide
his horse and to
safely scan the
countryside. He
saw in the distance
a large war party
going by at a
steady trot.

As the wolf
continued to
travel with the
warrior, he drew
his tail between
his legs and fled

three more times. Each time there was close danger at hand, and each time the wolf's warning saved his life. With the help of the wolf the Omaha warrior made his way to his village and arrived home unharmed.

What is now Ohio and Indiana was originally the home to the Omaha Indians. Then they moved west to Nebraska where they still live in the northeastern part of that state. The Omaha Indians are very closely related to the Osage Tribe, who lived along the Osage River near the lower course of the Ohio River in what is now Indiana, Kentucky, and Illinois. Later they moved west to Missouri and Kansas. Today they live in Oklahoma.

THE WOLF AND THE RACCOON
AND HOW
THE RED BIRDS
GOT THEIR COLOR
Cherokee and Seneca

A Raccoon walked by a Wolf one day poking fun at the Wolf as he passed. The Wolf became angry and quickly turned to chase the Raccoon. But the clever Raccoon ran swiftly to a tree on the river bank before the Wolf could catch him. The Raccoon climbed up the tree and, with great confidence, stretched himself on a limb overhanging the river. When the Wolf arrived, he looked for the Raccoon in the river. Then seeing the Raccoon's reflection in the water he jumped into the river to catch him, but he was just seeing the Raccoon's reflection and so he did not catch him.

After nearly drowning, the Wolf lay on
the bank of the river to dry and fell into
a deep sleep. While he was sleeping, the
Raccoon slipped down the tree and plas-
tered the Wolf's eyes closed with pine tar.
When the Wolf awoke he could not open
his eyes and began to cry for help.

Through the bushes came a little brown
bird who heard the Wolf crying.
He came up to the Wolf and
asked what was the matter.
So the Wolf told the little
brown bird the story of
how the Raccoon had out-
witted him. At the end
of his story the Wolf
told the little brown
bird, "If you will

help me get my eyes open, I will show you where to find some nice red paint to paint yourself." Being just a little brown bird he of course said, "Yes" and pecked at the Wolf's eyes until all the pine tar was gone.

True to his word, the Wolf took the little brown bird to a rock that had streaks of bright red paint running through it. The little bird painted himself with the red paint. Ever since that time he has no longer been the little brown bird but the beautiful Redbird.

The Cherokee, as mentioned above, lived in what is now the Southeastern United States. The Seneca Indians occupied what is now western New York State between Seneca Lake and the Geneva River. Many of the Seneca people still live in New York state and some also live in Oklahoma.

MEDICINE WOLVES AND COYOTES
Pawnee

One day as a man was walking alone he met a Coyote. Coyote spoke to the man and said, "How would you like to smoke my peace pipe?" The man thanked the Coyote and told him that yes he would like to smoke it. After the man had smoked he returned the pipe and the Coyote said to him: "You have smoked my peace pipe so now you are my friend and I will not harm you, but will take you to meet my people. I want my people to know that you have smoked my pipe. They will be glad to see you and will give you great powers."

They walked on a way, and
after a while they met many
Coyotes and Wolves. When the
Coyotes and the Wolves saw
the Coyote with the man, one
Wolf called to the other Wolves
and said: "Everyone be seated.
Let us hear what these people
who are coming have to say."

When they were seated the Coyote stood
up and said: "This man is my brother.
He smoked my pipe. He came with me
to pay you a visit. Let us take pity on him
and make him a wonderful man." The
man was frightened, for the Wolves came
very close to him. Then the man was
told that he must not be afraid to look.

So he did and saw many Coyotes, old and young. The Coyotes began to roll in the dust, then they came to the man and gave him plant roots and told him that the roots were good for healing the sick. Then one of the Coyotes arose and said: "We will give you this root and if any man is bitten by a mad dog give this medicine to him. He will then get well and not go mad. The other medicinal roots are good for other ailments and pains."

Next a Wolf stood up and rolled in the dust. Then he arose and gave the man a whistle and said: "I give you the whistle. When anybody is sick, use this whistle and the person will be made well." Then another Wolf arose and gave the man a piece of bone with the skull of a Wolf on it and he said: "Take this piece of bone. If anyone attempts to poison or bewitch you, lay the bone on your forehead and you will be able to overcome them. My power is in the bone."

Finally the man spoke and said: "This is enough. I thank you Wolves and Coyotes, I am glad I came here." Then Coyote took the man back to his village. "When you get home," the

Coyote said, "take this whistle. Blow it before you get home. Blow hard and we will hear it; all the Coyotes and Wolves will hear it." The man did as he was told and heard the Coyotes and Wolves howl in the distance.

After several days he heard of a man who was very ill. He went to him and doctored him. With the new healing powers he had learned from the Wolves and the Coyotes, he was able to cure the sick man.

The Pawnees once lived on the plains where Nebraska and eastern Wyoming are today. Their home is now in Pawnee, Oklahoma.

THE TIRED WOLF

Tlingit

One day, when the men of the Wolf Clan were out fishing, far from the shore, they saw a dark shadow moving in the water a great distance from them. They paddled quickly toward it and found a Wolf swimming so slowly that it hardly moved in the water. Its eyes were closed, and the poor Wolf was so tired that its tongue hung out. The animal could hardly keep its head above water. Friendly hands pulled the Wolf into the canoe, and the men of the Wolf Clan took the Wolf to their village.

For many years the Wolf lived with them. It always hunted with the men who had saved its life. Because the Wolf was a hunter he could always find trails to where deer and other animals could be found. The clan never lacked for meat. The Wolf lived with its rescuers for so long that the people began to think of it as a member of the clan.

One day the old Wolf lay on a mat in front of the house of the clan chief. Its friends gathered sadly around the Wolf, for they knew that the Wolf was very old and was about to take the Shadow Trail. Just as the sun sank, the old Wolf died.

The next night, a man of the clan heard
its relatives singing a death song for one
of their own. Their voices rose and fell
in a wailing song of mourning which filled
the forest with sadness.

From then on the clan adopted the song
of the Wolves as a mourning song. They
also decided from then on to carve the
figure of the tired Wolf on all of their
totem poles.

*The Tlingit Indians lived and fished
along the southern
coast of what is now
the state of
Alaska. Many
still live in
villages in
the same
region.*

THE WOLF
TEACHES MAGICAL SKILLS
Dakota Sioux

Once upon a time a man found a wolf den and decided to dig and get the cubs. The worried mother Wolf came barking and said to him, "Pity my children." But the man took no heed. The mother quickly ran to get the father of the cubs who came at once to confront the man. But the man ignored the Wolf father also and continued to dig the cubs out from the den. Frustrated, the father Wolf sang a beautiful song, "O man pity my children and I will teach you one of my magical skills." He ended his plea with a penetrating howl that caused a thick fog to cover the land. Then the Wolf howled again and the fog quickly disappeared.

Awed by the Wolf's gift, the man reconsidered and did not steal the cubs. He thought to himself, "These animals have

mysterious gifts." So he tore up his red blanket into small pieces and made pretty Indian red cloth necklaces for the cubs and took the cubs back to their parents.

The father was so thankful that he made this promise to the man, "When you go into battle hereafter, I will accompany you, and bring to pass whatever you wish." Then they soon parted as friends.

In the course of time, the man went to battle against his enemies. As he came into sight of the enemy village, a large

Wolf met him saying, "By and by I will sing and you shall take their horses when they least expect it." So the man and the Wolf stopped on a hill close to the enemy village. Fulfilling his promise, the Wolf sang his song. After this he howled making a high wind arise. The horses fled to the forest, many stopping on the hillside. When the Wolf howled again, the wind

died away and a
mist arose. So the
man, under the
cover of the mist,
took as many horses
as he wished.

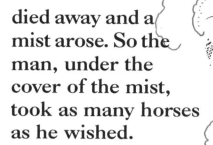

*The Sioux once occupied more
territory than any other Indian
tribe. More recently, they moved
from the western Great Lakes area
to what is now Nebraska, North
Dakota, and South Dakota. Most of
the Sioux people now live in North
Dakota and South Dakota.*

PRINCE OF THE WOLVES
Tsimshian

The long, pitiful howl of a timber Wolf came from the forest behind the village. The people of the village were afraid and hungry. The winter food supply was almost gone and there was little left to eat. The people thought perhaps the Wolves were hungry too, maybe hungry enough to attack the village. They listened fearfully, but heard only the loud pitiful wail of one Wolf.

A young chief who was not afraid of the Wolf said he would go to the forest and see why the Wolf howled. He took his bow and arrows and went. He worked his way through the thick undergrowth, toward the place where the Wolf wailed.

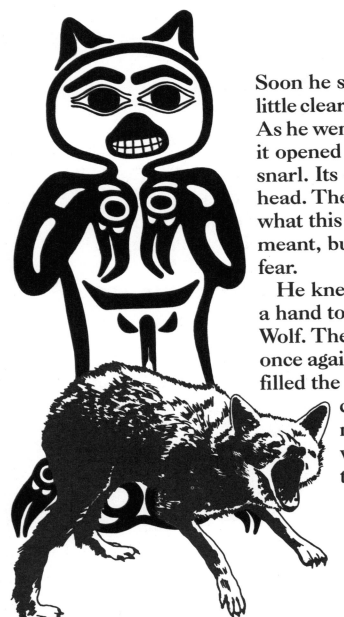

Soon he saw the Wolf in a little clearing in front of him. As he went toward the Wolf, it opened its mouth in a snarl. Its ears lay flat on its head. The young chief knew what this danger signal meant, but he showed no fear.

He knelt down and held a hand toward the wary Wolf. The snarl stopped and once again a mournful howl filled the forest. The Wolf came nearer and nearer until it was within reach of the young chief.